My Visit With Jesus of Nazareth

By

Asbury H. Williams

Copyright © 2006 by Asbury H. Williams

My Visit With Jesus of Nazareth
by Asbury H. Williams

Printed in the United States of America

ISBN 1-60034-712-6

All rights reserved solely by the author. The author guarantees all contents are original and do not infringe upon the legal rights of any other person or work. No part of this book may be reproduced in any form without the permission of the author. The views expressed in this book are not necessarily those of the publisher.

Unless otherwise indicated, Bible quotations are taken from:

The King James Bible – no copyright

The New Revised Standard Bible - copyright © 1997 by World Bible Publishers, Inc.

The Living Bible - copyright © 1971 by Tyndale House Publishers

www.xulonpress.com

Introduction

For the past four years, I have been planning and thinking about this short book. While it is a work of fiction, I feel deeply that God has led me to write this story. Please don't stop in the middle! Keep reading it to the end. I think that you will receive a blessing when you read this story about "My Visit With Jesus of Nazareth".

I dedicate this writing to my dear friend, Rev. J. Kirk Lawton, Jr. who has helped me with my research and made some excellent suggestions. I also dedicate this writing to my loving wife of 47 years, Peggy, whom I love very deeply, my family (3 children and 4 grandchildren), and my friends at Timberlake Baptist Church.

Asbury H. Williams

September, 2006

Prologue

Every person I have met has become a part of me. My parents and siblings, certainly – my teachers and classmates in kindergarten, grade school, middle school, college and postgraduate school are also obvious, as are my social friends. There are others who are not so obvious. I have been influenced by every waitress, every check out person, every bank teller, every car salesman, every performing musician, the cab driver in New York who didn't know the way to the airport, perhaps even the subliminal encounters with people I pass on the sidewalk or see in an elevator. Each of these has had a miniscule influence on who I am. My personality is a sum of my genes, my upbringing, and all of the people I have encountered, even transiently, during my lifetime. Each has had their influence on who I am. And most of all, I have been influenced by my wonderful wife, with whom I have shared so much.

And then there was the pigeon. Every time I feel depressed, I think about that pigeon. It was a cold winter day. I was sitting in a restaurant having lunch with my wife and two other couples. There were several pigeons sitting on a wire outside the restaurant. Some would leave and others would land on the wire and sit for a few minutes, but there was one pigeon that kept standing on his right leg and not moving. I kept looking at that pigeon. I couldn't see his left leg. Had he lost his left leg? Had he injured it so that it was so painful that he couldn't put any weight on it? My eyes kept going back to that poor pigeon. He had a forlorn appearance. How long could he stand on one leg? It was cold and windy. When would a predator attack him? I watched that blasted pigeon for about forty-five minutes and he never moved. I still wonder today how long he lasted. Did he make it through that day and into the night? Probably not.

How many people in this world are like that pigeon? They are crippled and living in a society that makes no provision for them. I wish I could forget seeing that pigeon, but that forlorn image keeps coming back in my mind. It's been over 10 years and I'm still influenced by that brave, suffering pigeon.

Chapter 1

My name is Hamilton Pearson, BS, MS, and PhD. I grew up in a small South Carolina agricultural town and attended a fundamentalist Baptist church until I left home to go to college. The church was our main social meeting place and my family took me there every Sunday morning and Wednesday evening. I accepted their basic religious beliefs as part of my Christian upbringing, but when I started my college education, I began to look at things from a different point of view. I had made straight A's all though school and I had no problems making straight A's in college even though I was attending one of the top ten universities in the country and had a very tough schedule. I was one of only twenty students in the country who made a perfect SAT score of 1600. I was found to have an IQ of over 200 using multiple tests. I had been awarded full scholarships by ten different major universities before I made my final choice. I plunged quickly into the stratospheric academic atmosphere of the university. I took every science and mathematics course that I could squeeze into my schedule but I also began to question the basic religious beliefs I had accepted as a child.

Virgin birth? Resurrection from the dead? Walking on water? Healing withered limbs with a touch? Raising a man from the dead? Being crucified buried and resurrected on the third day? My practical scientific mind could no longer accept these beliefs. I stopped attending church during the first month of my freshman year and I began to look with disdain at the superstitious people who attended church faithfully week after week, stubbornly believing in two thousand year old scripture. My life was in the present, not in some past happenings of dubious credibility.

After I obtained my PhD degree, I plunged into my work. The scientific community began to recognize that I was someone with special talents. I became world famous for my work in the fields of computer science, aerospace technology, and quantum physics. I began doing innovative studies often working over 12 hours a day, seven days a week. People who worked with me thought that I was being driven by a desire to benefit the people of the world and that was partially true, but there was a secondary reason for my zeal that I shared with no one. My real driving force was to show the world once and for all what really happened during the thirty-three short years of Jesus' life. I wanted with all my heart and mind, (I didn't believe in souls), to prove to the world that these things were simply myths –myths that had been taken in by millions of gullible people over the past 2000 years.

I thought that if the world could discard these myths and spend just half of the energy and money being thrown away by these so called "Christians," we could convert this time and energy into doing constructive things for the people of the earth. We could improve the lives of our society in a useful and meaningful way. Our world could be so much better. We could do away with hunger and poverty. We could find alternative fuels and save the planet that we were systematically destroying. We could find new innovative medical cures. I watched the different Christian denominations arguing and fighting with one another over petty differences. I saw infighting in many churches over small issues that no one would be able to remember one hundred years from now. I saw evangelists pretending to heal the sick in front of millions of faithful people who were watching on TV, and always, always asking for more and more money. I was disgusted with the whole mess!

When I was twenty-five, I began tinkering with the idea of time travel. It can look easy in the movies, but in reality, it is incredibly complex. You see, our earth is not only moving in orbit around our sun while it rotates on its axis; the sun is also moving slowly as our universe expands. When one attempts to travel in time, one must also travel in space. My first time travel machine was a vertical take off and landing jet plane that the U.

S. military had been developing but later decided to abandon. I was able to buy it for a relatively low price. My wife and my fellow workers thought that I had lost my mind, because the plane was incredibly expensive to operate. No one but my wife knew of my real plans. The plane I had chosen had some similarities to the British Harrier, but it would accommodate four passengers rather than two plus accommodating a significant load of equipment. I quickly learned how to fly the plane and began using my aerospace engineering experience to modify the plane for space travel. I began by installing my tiny proprietary computers that were light years ahead of anything available commercially. My progress was very slow, due both to the incredible complexities involved in this innovative project and my duties with my work. After five years of work on the machine, I was able to move forward or backward in time for one to two minutes. As my equipment became more sophisticated, I learned how to move in time for one to two week periods, then one to two month periods, and finally I learned to move forward or backward for one or two years at a time. I became super rich investing in the stock market by knowing what and when to sell. I would fly forward for a few weeks, read the newspapers, then fly back to the time period I had left. I would buy stocks that I knew would be worth a lot more in a short period of time. I threw in some losses as well as short and long-term gains to avoid suspicion. I didn't want to be investigated by the Securities and Exchange Commission.

Chapter Two

Over the years I had upgraded and improved the reliability of my equipment. Now I was thirty-four years old and ready to go back to the time of Jesus. I knew that I had to go while I was still relatively young and in good shape because the physical exertion would be much more than I had ever experienced. But first I had to find the right people to go with me. I needed an expert on the languages of that period of history. I have given scientific lectures in French, Spanish, and German, but I have no training or experience with ancient languages. I needed a very reputable physician/scientist to study the so-called miracles. I also needed a religious expert in Christianity who was universally respected and whom few would question. We would take small digital video cameras with us to document our findings. Now I needed to begin recruiting the right people to travel with me on this epic journey.

All of my recruits had to be multi-talented. I could take only four travelers including myself. Someone beside myself would have to learn to fly and maintain my machine. Needless to say, I needed people with a very rare combination of talents. In addition to their talents, my travel companions had to be relatively young and in very good health. They needed to be men because of the mores of that period of time. They couldn't be too tall, because the average height of a person that long ago was shorter than now, and I didn't want us to stand out any more than possible.

My first contact would be at Furman University in Greenville, South Carolina, only fifty miles from my home. Furman was originally a Baptist college and was supported by the South Carolina Baptist Convention for over a hundred years before becoming independent. Furman had been located in the downtown area of Greenville for over a hundred years, but with no room to expand, they bought a large tract of land north of Greenville in the 1950's. Long-range plans were made for the new campus. Landscaping experts led by an experienced supervisor from England were hired to plan the campus landscaping far into the future. The sites for the dormitories, classrooms, library, chapel, athletics, and all other buildings were planned for over fifty years in advance. This resulted in one of the most beautiful university campuses in the country. The first class to graduate from the new campus was the class of 1959. As I drove my BMW 750 north of Greenville, I looked up at Paris Mountain ahead on my right, covered with radio and TV antennas. I saw the turnoff to Furman University on the right and was carried under the highway to the campus entrance. As I entered the beautiful campus, I went around a traffic circle with a large fountain in the center. I noticed that all of the buildings were matched in style and the exteriors were made from red Virginia bricks.

I arrived about thirty minutes early, so I decided to drive around the campus. There was a large lake right behind the library with some small boats and canoes on the banks. Behind the lake was an old bell tower, which had been moved from the old campus. The landscaping was beautiful. I parked and began walking toward the classroom building where the history department was located. When I walked past students, most of them smiled and said hello. I had never seen a happier campus.

The history department was located in one of the older classroom buildings. I was to meet Dr. Adrian Jenkins, a visiting professor who had a national reputation as an expert in the period of history we were going to visit. He also had an extensive knowledge of the languages spoken and written during that period. I walked in to the ground floor of the two-story building and was directed to Dr. Jenkins' office by a friendly student. I walked up one flight of stairs and easily found his office on the second floor. The door was closed and I knocked on it. I expected a receptionist, but heard a quick "come on in" from a male voice, and I walked into a cramped office. The office was smaller than I expected and I was surprised to see that the bookshelves were not crammed with books. Actually the office was very neat and well organized, with a minimum number of books and magazines. As my eyes scanned the room, I noted a state of the art Sony mainframe computer against the concrete wall along with a high end Canon multifunction printer/scanner/copy/fax machine.

Dr. Jenkins stood quickly and gave me a firm handshake, looking directly into my eyes. His eyes were dark brown and he wore a dark brown beard. He had agreed to an appointment with me based on my reputation, but I knew that he had to have a great deal of curiosity as to why a world famous physicist would want to meet with him. While shaking my hand he again looked into my eyes and with a smile he said, "You must be Dr. Pearson. I've been looking forward to meeting you, but I can't imagine why you would want to meet with me!"

I liked his directness. He was obviously a no-nonsense person. He was about 5 feet 10 inches tall. His hair and beard were well groomed. There were no gray hairs that I could see. His upper front teeth were slightly crooked. That was good. The people we were going to see did not have dentists and their teeth would be far from perfect. His beard was just what we needed for our travel journey, although we would have to let it grow out more and become scruffier. He invited me to sit down in a small office chair, the only other chair in the room besides his desk chair. He turned to a coffee maker and offered me a cup of coffee, which I accepted gratefully.

After a few preliminary pleasantries, I began to ask him some questions. "Dr. Jenkins, I'm trying to learn some information about the period of history in which Jesus lived and about the languages spoken in that part of the world during that period of time? I'm hoping that you can enlighten me about that era." He was obviously surprised by my question, but quickly began to offer me some information. "Most scholars believe that Jesus was probably born in about 3 BC and lived until about 30 AD. The reason for this seemingly contradictory dating is because of an error in the early Roman calendar. Jesus is generally believed to have been crucified at the age of 33 after only a three-year ministry." I nodded my understanding, encouraging him to go ahead. "The primary languages spoken during that period were probably Greek and Aramaic. Hebrew was generally used only in the Jewish temples during formal worship services. And off course, with the Romans ruling the area, Latin was also spoken or understood by many people. Jesus probably spoke a mixture of Aramaic and Greek as did many people of that time."

I decided to be very direct and interrupted him quickly. "Dr. Jenkins, if a person were able to travel back to that period of time and if that person were an expert in the languages of that time, would he be able to understand what was being said?" Dr. Jenkins stared at me with a whimsical look for what seemed like an eternity before answering. I could almost see the wheels turning in his head. Finally he answered. "The quick answer is, 'no one knows'. As you know, in our culture today, languages are transmitted all over the world by radio, TV, and telephone. In Jesus' time, of course, that type of communication did not exist. Even in more modern times, the Chinese had over 1000 dialects within their country. We have no real idea of how many dialects might have been spoken in the holy land 2000 years ago. People, of course, were much more separated from one another than they are today."

I decided to continue to be direct and hit him between the eyes with my proposal. "Dr. Jenkins, you know my reputation as a scientist. I have patents on many inventions. I have been nominated for a Nobel Prize in physics but came in 3rd in the final vote. I'm telling you this so that you won't think I've lost my mind when I tell you what I am contemplating. Over the past ten years I've developed a time/space travel machine. I've been going backward in time briefly for several years and I've gradually been expanding the period of time that I can reach. I'm now ready to travel back to the time of Jesus and see him in person. I'm inviting you to travel with me."

I expected to see an expression of shock on Dr. Jenkins' face, but he only looked at me with a bemused expression. Finally he spoke. "I've been sitting here trying to imagine what you could possibly want from me. You could have obtained the historical information I gave you from many sources including the Internet. I'll have to say that your proposal to travel back in time never entered my mind, but knowing your reputation, I'm not that surprised. But as much as I would like to go with you, I can't just walk away from my job."

I smiled at him. "You don't have to miss even a day of work! You see, we can go back in time for two or three weeks and I can return you to the exact date in time that you left! No one will even know you've been gone!"

Chapter 3

After securing my first recruit, I had more confidence. After all, what person could resist the chance to go back in time and see Jesus in person? The second person I wanted to recruit was a physician at the Duke University School of Medicine. Walter Bonner, M. D. is an expert in rare and exotic diseases. He is one of the few physicians in the United States who has ever seen an advanced case of leprosy. He has traveled all over the world where leprosy – now known as Hansen's disease - still exists. Hansen's disease has been almost eliminated in the United States. Since leprosy was apparently prevalent during Jesus' lifetime, I wanted to take someone with me who could verify the diagnosis. I also wanted a reputable physician who could evaluate any other so-called miracles.

Dr. Bonner's office was not actually located in the Duke University Hospital, or the Duke campus. He was located in an ultra-modern high-rise building in city of Durham.

Durham is a city of about two hundred thousand people and is the proud home of the research triangle. Dr. Bonner's office building looked as if it was only two or three years old. I checked the directory in the lobby and saw that his office was on the third floor. I took the immaculate elevator up to his floor, gave my name to his receptionist, and proceeded to sit down and wait in the reception area for over an hour before I was finally called back to a spacious modern office. The office was empty and I cooled my heels for another thirty minutes until the door opened and Dr. Bonner rushed in. He was clearly distracted and gave me the impression that he was gracing me with his presence. I have little tolerance for self-important people and I began to fume. He looked at his watch and gave me a limp handshake. “I’m Doctor Bonner, what can I do for you?” He didn’t make eye contact. I was livid. “Dr. Bonner, I’ve traveled a long way to see you. You promised me that I would be able to have two hours of your undivided attention. You’ve kept me waiting for over an hour and a half and you keep looking at your watch like you don’t want to waste your time with me. So are you going to give me the time you promised me or not?” Dr.

Bonner sat down heavily in his chair. "I'm sorry, Dr. Pearson, I just lost a young patient. She wasn't thought to be in any danger. We were working her up for a chronic infectious condition. She was in X-Ray getting ready to have a routine film made and she suddenly went into cardiac arrest.

A code blue was called and there was a quick response. Everything possible was done to resuscitate her and nothing worked. I try not to let things get to me, but this was totally unexpected. I walked out into the waiting room not knowing how to tell the parents. They gave me a big smile and said "Hi, Dr.

Bonner." What did you find? Then they saw the look on my face and realized that something was terribly wrong. I had to take them back and tell them that their sixteen-year-old daughter had died while getting a routine chest X-Ray.

I could now see that Dr. Bonner was a caring, compassionate physician. They seem to be few and far between. More and more physicians try not to allow themselves to get emotional about their patients, but none of them can completely suppress their feelings. Those suppressed feelings can eat away at them for years. Some of them retire early, some take tranquillizers or antidepressants, some divorce their spouses, some do totally irrational things with their lives, and some commit suicide. Dr. Bonner appeared to be in his mid thirties. He was obviously in excellent physical condition. Like Dr. Pearson, he also had brown hair and a brown beard. I couldn't believe my good fortune!

I talked with Dr. Bonner about his experiences with leprosy and other infectious diseases. I knew that in ancient times other severe skin infections might have been called leprosy. Dr. Bonner talked for a while about his experiences and the current treatments of

Hansen's disease. He told about how sulfones were used at one time but are currently not used because of newer and better medications. I asked him about his trips to India, Korea, and other countries where Hansen's disease is still found. His experiences were heart breaking and I could see that he had a real zeal in taking care of these patients.

I finally broached my proposal to go to the holy land in Jesus' time. It took me only thirty minutes to persuade him to join my expedition into what most Christians believe to be the greatest three years in the history of mankind. Dr. Bonner would probably have a chance to see more types of serious infectious diseases in our three-week journey than he would see during his entire life. He was eager to join us in our expedition.

Chapter Four

My third candidate needed to be a Christian minister who was also a pilot, an engineer, and who was totally credible. I needed to teach him how to pilot my time machine for obvious reasons. I couldn't take on such a task solely by myself. There were too many things to be done, too many bad things that could happen. I knew that navigation was going to be a large obstacle when we went back 2000 years in time. There would be no communication satellites or GPS satellites. There would be no radio beacons. Even finding the holy land itself could present a major problem.

James Martin Covington is a famous evangelical minister. Unlike many of today's televangelists, he and his ministry have never had a whisper of scandal. Like Billy Graham, he never asks for money. He is affiliated with a major protestant denomination. He travels all over the world spreading the gospel of Jesus Christ. He is also an excellent pilot, often taking over the controls of his corporate

Learjet. He had been a nominal Christian for most of his life, but after graduating from college, he had a spiritual experience, which led him to enroll in the George W. Truett Theological Seminary where he obtained his Master of Theological Studies and Doctor of Ministry degrees. In addition to his theological degrees, he also has a college degree in aerospace engineering, which he obtained from North Carolina State University. His home base is in western North Carolina not far from Black Mountain. As you can see, I was trying to recruit people who lived in relatively close proximity to me so that we could minimize our travel time during our preparations.

I caught up with Dr. Covington in London where he was speaking to packed audiences. I had made an appointment to see him at his hotel after his evening service. He was very pleasant and down to earth. Like my other candidates, he too was in his mid thirties. That had been another of my criteria in choosing my travel mates. The average life expectancy 2000 years ago was much shorter than it is now. Our travelers needed to fit into a narrow age group. They also had to be in very good physical condition. We were going to be doing a lot of walking in a hostile climate.

Dr. Covington also had a medium brown beard with a few flecks of gray. He was about 5 feet 11 inches tall and his eyes were brown. His teeth were almost too perfect. We would have to do some sort of camouflage there. He had a deep cultured voice. There was something about him that I couldn't put my finger on. He seemed to be preoccupied and did not initially make eye contact. I began giving him my spiel and he brightened up considerably. He appeared to be more fascinated with my proposed trip than either of my other candidates. I put it down to the fact that he was a Christian minister. He quickly agreed to travel with us on our historic journey. I now had my full team of time travelers.

Chapter 5

We began our training by going back in time for weekend intervals. We would meet at a private airport in the northern part of South Carolina that was a convenient drive for each of us. We would use my time machine to go back in time for three or four days. Then we traveled to various desolate desert areas and wore the sandals and clothing of the Roman era. Fortunately for us, the styles of that day didn't change frequently like they do now and we had plenty of documents demonstrating the types of clothing that were worn. We slept outdoors in the desert directly on the ground as we began getting gradually acclimated to the hot days and cold nights. We didn't use tents or sleeping bags. We wanted to sleep like we would have to sleep on our journey. We let our beards grow out more and they became shaggier. We gradually let our skins tan. We began eating dried dates and figs, lamb and fish, and other foods common to that era. We realized that we would never be able to pass ourselves off as locals. The best that we could hope for was that we would be accepted as contemporary foreigners who had strange looks, a strange language, and strange customs. We would speak to one another quietly in English. We spent over three months preparing ourselves for our journey. We had regular meetings, studied diligently and tried to prepare for any eventuality. We had some crude coins made out of gold and silver. We would carry small digital video cameras camouflaged as much as reasonably possible. We knew that we couldn't hide everything. We would just have to be four strange foreigners who stayed around for three weeks and then disappeared.

We considered taking weapons with us, but we would be afraid to kill anyone, even in self-defense. We were acutely aware of the potential "butterfly effect" that could happen if we killed one person or even one animal or insect. One small mishap could potentially change the course of history. We had no idea what even the slightest mistake on our part could have on the future. At the same time, we couldn't allow ourselves to be killed 2000 years in the past leaving our bodies and our time/space travel machine 2000 years before we were born. We finally settled on carrying stun guns to use defensively if we faced a life or death situation. We bought the stun guns and began learning how to use them. We spent a great deal of time checking out our other equipment.

*　*　*

Dr. Covington sat alone in his bedroom reading his Bible and praying. He felt a deep sense of guilt about hiding his medical condition from the other three time travelers. Only two days before being approached by Dr.

Pearson, he had learned that he had a very rare and incurable form of cancer. He would retain his energy level for about one year, and then his health would begin to deteriorate rapidly. There was absolutely no doubt about his diagnosis. He would have jumped at the opportunity to go on this trip under any circumstances, but he was hoping against hope for a miraculous healing from Jesus. His thoughts wandered back to his pleasant days at the George W. Truett Seminary, which is affiliated with Baylor University. He had enjoyed his time there. Now he had succeeded beyond his wildest dreams in just a few short years, but he had so much more that he needed to do. All of his hopes depended on seeing Jesus in person.

Chapter 6

After weeks of preparation, the time for our departure had finally arrived. All of our plans had been made down to the last detail. One of my major concerns was setting off alarms from the spy satellites when we flew into space. Our previous trips in time had been for only a few days or weeks at a time. We were now going to travel two thousand years back in time. This trip would be a much more complex endeavor. I finally decided that our departure should be from a fairly remote area of South America where our departure would be less likely to be noticed. We would take off and fly toward the South Pole and then we would just disappear from any curious radar screens. We would try to re-enter the earth's atmosphere in the year 28 AD, and travel from the lower part of Africa northward up to the Holy Land. Our target would be Lake Gennesaret – known in the Bible as the Sea of Galilee. We knew that Jesus had supposedly spent a great deal of time in that area during his ministry.

We all arranged to take a one-week vacation at the same time. My original promise that we would leave and return on the same day without missing work was thwarted by our need to leave from South America. I managed to have my machine transferred in advance to a remote area of Patagonia in the lower part of South America. All of us flew on Varig Airlines from Miami to Rio. The Boeing 747 had spacious seats and fresh cut flowers in the toilets. Liquor was being poured out of large bottles rather than mini bottles. Of course all of us abstained. Even if we had been drinkers, we wouldn't have wanted to take anything into our bodies that could affect our concentration or our reflexes. The pilot made his announcements in Portuguese, Spanish, and English. I tried on the music headphones supplied on the plane and was surprised to hear Chet Baker playing the trumpet and singing. Most people my age have never heard of him. He's been dead for over fifteen years. I know this makes me old fashioned, but Chet had always been a favorite of mine. I would often play some of his smooth jazz while I worked on my projects.

After spending the night in a 4 star hotel in Rio, we flew a much smaller plane farther south and inland to our remote airport location. All of us were nervous and excited as we checked our equipment. We had four digital video cameras – two to digital tapes, and two directly to mini DVD disks. We also had still cameras – both film and digital. We had foods, medicines, a few liquid drinks, water sterilization pills, and all kinds of scientific tools, but we could carry only so much. Our time travel machine also had built-in cameras to document our flight over Africa to the Holy Land. We took off at 3 AM local time in order to attract as little attention as possible. We flew over Antarctica and went through our time warp as planned, suddenly finding ourselves flying over the southern part of Africa heading north.

I had flown over Africa before and the difference was incredible. The southern part of Africa appeared totally green. There were no buildings, roads, or any signs of civilization to be seen except for an occasional small plume of smoke. The ocean on our left was incredibly blue, not the polluted ocean we had become accustomed to seeing in the 21st century. As we approached northern Africa, we could begin to see some desert areas, but they appeared smaller than when I had seen them in the 21st century. At least with the desert area, we were able to see the ground and we began to identify some small settlements.

Looking at the ground, I was also able to see some rivers. Our computerized scanners were trying to recognize some general terrain features that I had placed in their data banks and began comparing their major features with data from the 21st century. We quickly had a lock on the Nile River and saw the pyramids to our left. Our scanners began looking for major cities. They found Cairo near the pyramids almost immediately, and then our computers pinpointed Jerusalem, Bethlehem, the Sea of Galilee, the Dead Sea, and the remote area we were looking for in order to land our craft. We wanted a desolate area where travelers were unlikely to be. It needed to be within relatively easy walking distance to the Sea of Galilee. This would be our first goal on our momentous journey. We found a remote, uninhabited area roughly ten miles from the Sea of Galilee and landed without incident. We quickly put desert camouflage over our craft and made sure that we had all of our equipment, including simple food, water, and medicines. We knew that later on we would have to obtain our food from the local inhabitants.

We checked our magnetic compasses and began our travel on foot. It didn't take us long to realize just how hot this desert really was. The desert training areas that we had used in the United States seemed mild in comparison to what we were experiencing. We began to perspire profusely. Our extensive conditioning at home had not begun to prepare us for this hostile climate. As night approached, we camped out and tried to rest. The temperature dropped quickly and we had to wrap ourselves in our blankets. We were very careful to carry our trash with us and to be sure that we did no harm to any animals – even insects. We had no idea how even the simplest changes we made in time could affect the future. We wanted to avoid "the butterfly effect."

Chapter 7

After several hours of fitful sleep on the desert sand, we continued on our journey. Soon, we began to notice some fellow travelers. All of them stared at us intensely. Even though we had done all that we could think of to fit into their culture, we knew that we would appear obviously different from them. For one thing, our clothing was too new and clean. This was something that we had overlooked in our preparations. We could only hope to try to continue our journey in peace.

After about four more hours of walking, we began to see life ahead of us. Flying birds became more prevalent. We began to see an ever-increasing number of people. Most of them seemed to be heading in the same direction as we. Many of them appeared obviously excited. There was a tension in the air that we had not noticed before. Soon we reached the shore of the Sea of Galilee.

We knew that one side of the Sea of Galilee formed a natural amphitheater and we saw dozens of people taking their seats. They were sitting on the ground in the amphitheater facing the shore. We selected an unoccupied area about halfway down the incline where people were sitting and took our seats. We received numerous stares from the people, but they appeared friendly and there was no evidence of animosity. Most of them were chattering away with one another. All of them appeared to be excited. We all pulled out our mini camcorders and we made sure that they were working.

Soon after the four of us took our seats, a small group of men approached the shore in a fishing boat rigged with sails and fishing nets. The boat landed on the shore and all of the men stepped out. One man was obviously in charge and the others were very deferential to him. The leader approached a spot that was not far from the shore and looked up at the amphitheater, which was becoming more and more crowded with people. He began slowly moving his eyes across the gathering crowd. Soon he made eye contact with me. I returned his look and he held my gaze for a few seconds before moving his eyes across the rest of the crowd. I had never experienced a feeling like this in my life! I heard a stir in the crowd. Everyone seemed to be murmuring to one another. They were feeling the same thing that I had felt. This man was not just looking into my eyes; he was looking into my soul!

To this day it is still hard for me to describe this man. His long hair was a medium brown. His beard was the same color and relatively short compared to the other men around him. He had the kindest expression on his face that I have ever seen! He appeared to be relaxed and completely at ease. He sat there patiently until the crowd began to quiet down. Soon, he held up his right hand and all noise in the crowd immediately ceased. We didn't even hear a baby cry or a child making noises. The man began to speak softly and gently. His voice carried to us and could be heard easily. Of course I couldn't understand a word that he was saying. After the man had talked for about five minutes, I turned and looked at Dr. Jenkins. He had the most stunned expression on his face that I had ever seen. I tried to get his attention, but he quickly waved me off. After speaking for about 30 minutes, the man stood up and held out his arms.

Chapter 8

Many people in the crowd stood up and began to walk down toward the man who had been speaking. I quickly grabbed Dr. Jenkins. "What was the man saying," I said. Dr. Jenkins had an expression of happiness beyond description. He was very excited. "It took me a few minutes to figure out what he was saying. He was talking mostly in Aramaic, but he occasionally used a Greek or Latin word. He was saying, "Blessed are the poor in spirit, for theirs is the kingdom of heaven". I stared at Dr. Jenkins. I had had enough religious training in my childhood to realize that the speaker was Jesus himself and he was preaching the "Sermon on the Mount'" which includes The Beatitudes. Dr. Jenkins said, "That was where he started, but he gave the entire Sermon on the Mount almost word for word like it appears in the Bible."

We joined the crowd moving down toward Jesus. Many of them were obviously sick. Jesus was touching and praying for them one by one. They would each stand up and leave, many of them leaping up and down with joy. Their families were standing with them raising their hands toward heaven. I saw Jesus touch one man whose right arm was severely withered and the arm immediately became normal! I noticed Dr. Covington making his way down toward Jesus and I saw Jesus touch him and pray for him. I quickly made sure that all of us were recording this with our cameras. I couldn't believe my eyes and wanted to carry these moving pictures back to the 21st century.

How could this be! I have one of the best scientific minds in the world. I had explained many previously unexplained scientific problems. I thought that I had an explanation for everything, but I had no scientific explanation for any of this! It was beyond logic! It was beyond science! It was beyond any explanation! There was no scientific basis for this! For the first time in my life, I was completely devoid of any logical explanation for what I had seen with my own eyes. I finally had to sit down. I began to cry uncontrollably. I didn't know my body was capable of making such a large amount of tears. After a few minutes of continuous crying, I felt a hand on my shoulder. Thinking it was one of my traveling companions; I looked up and found myself looking directly into the eyes of Jesus. Those eyes! Those eyes! He was still looking directly into my soul! He placed his right hand on the top of my head and turned his eyes upward to what I knew had to be heaven. I could sense that Jesus was praying for me. Praying for "ME", a man who had devoted much of his adult life trying to prove that he was a myth! After the prayer, Jesus looked into my eyes again and began speaking. I did not know what he was saying, but I felt a deep peace diffuse throughout my entire body. My inner being was more relaxed than it had ever been during my life. Then Jesus turned and walked slowly to the shore followed by his disciples. They boarded the fishing boat and cast off.

After Jesus left, I looked for my friends who were standing nearby watching me closely. They too were almost speechless. I finally found my voice and turned to Dr. Jenkins. "What did Jesus say to me?" Dr. Jenkins smiled at me. "He was saying, 'Let not your heart be troubled. You believe in God, believe also in me!'"

Chapter 9

I walked away from the area with a mixture of sadness and joy. I was sad because I had doubted Jesus for most of my life. But at the same time, I felt an inner peace and happiness that was far beyond anything I had ever experienced in my life. It went to the depth of my soul. One hour ago I didn't believe that souls existed. Now I had seen and heard Jesus! I had felt his hands placed upon my head! I had seen him perform miraculous healings! I had heard him pray for me and he was the real thing! He wasn't a fable. He wasn't a composite of people put together over the years. He wasn't a normal man. He wasn't a hoax. He wasn't an imposter. He was real! I needed no further proof! I understood that my life had changed forever in a milli-second of time! From that time forward, I would dedicate my life to serving Jesus and spreading his gospel. I couldn't wait to get home and show the recordings that we had made. No one could argue with this evidence. I had irrefutable proof that no one could deny.

We knew that we were standing on holy ground and none of us wanted to leave. Finally as sunset drew near, we walked away to find a place to rest. We found someone selling freshly cooked fish. He looked at our pieces of gold carefully and quickly gave us all of the fish we wanted. I could tell by the expression on his face that he was taking advantage of us. It didn't matter. What we had learned was worth far more than gold. Locals in the 21st century now refer to the fish that we were eating as "St. Peter's Fish". We were ravenous and the fish were delicious. We found a secluded spot nearby where we could sleep for the night. We quickly played back some of the scenes on our video cameras and again marveled at the miraculous healings. We wanted to be up early tomorrow. We couldn't wait to follow Jesus wherever he went.

As I lay there trying to fall asleep, a long dormant passage of scripture entered my mind. I hadn't read the Bible in over fifteen years and I was surprised to be able to remember scripture that I had been taught as a child and adolescent. The scripture that entered my mind was from Matthew 6. I couldn't remember the exact words but the verse went like this. “Don’t worry about your life, what you will eat or what you will drink, or about your body, what you will wear. Is not life more than food and the body more than clothing? Look at the birds in the air. They neither sow nor reap nor gather into barns, and yet your heavenly Father feeds them. And can any of you by worrying add a single hour to your life?” I began thinking about that poor pigeon that I had seen years ago bravely standing on his right leg. I realized that God watches over all of us and He loves us and wants the best for us. He's sad when we turn away from him.

I ended up crying myself to sleep.

*   *   *

Dr. Covington slept the best sleep he had slept in weeks. Jesus had prayed for him and touched him and he knew beyond a shadow of a doubt that his cancer was gone and that he was completely healed!

Chapter 10

We awoke at sunrise the next morning. Dr. Bonner was eager to see some people with leprosy and observe Jesus healing them. We saw Jesus eating breakfast with some of his disciples. We dug into our travel bags and ate some dates, washing them down with water that we had brought along with us. Soon, Jesus stood up and his disciples quickly followed suit. They began walking away from the resting area and we followed them at a discreet distance.

In a short time, we saw a small canyon ahead of us. A few people were standing on the edge of the canyon lowering food and water to the bottom. We arrived at the edge of the canyon and looked down. I will never forget the sight. A group of the most wretched people I had ever seen were standing at the bottom pushing and shoving each other to get to the food and water that was being lowered. Many others were apparently too weak to stand and remained recumbent, staring blankly at the others. All of the people in the canyon were covered with hideous sores. Many of them had lost some of their fingers and toes. They looked awful. Dr. Bonner looked at them for a while and turned to us. "Even from this distance, I can tell that many of them have leprosy, but I need to find a way down and look at them more closely."

Just then, we heard a commotion from Jesus' disciples. They were obviously arguing with Jesus. They were trying to stop him from going down into the canyon. Jesus didn't argue back. He simply turned and approached the edge of the canyon, looking closely. For the first time, I saw a path leading to the bottom of the canyon. Jesus began walking down the path, but the disciples were afraid to follow him. The four of us picked up our belongings and began following Jesus down the narrow path. The crowd really started to murmur when they saw us following him. When Jesus reached the bottom, the miserable people surged toward him. Jesus didn't try to avoid them. Instead, he began laying his hands on them and praying for them one at a time.

By that time, we were only a few feet up the path and could see everything happening right in front of us. As Jesus laid his hands on each of the wretched people, their deformities and the terrible sores began to disappear as if by magic. All of us had our video cameras recording as much as possible. We followed Jesus as he healed over 100 lepers. Dr. Bonner was speechless as were all of us! He examined many of the healed people very closely. There wasn't even a tiny scar left on any of them. We all realized that we were witnessing miracle after miracle with total and complete healing of the lepers. These men, women, and children who had been so sick with this hideous disease were completely healed!

They began picking up their meager belongings with a spring in their step and began walking up the path to the top of the canyon. Their families and friends at the top of the canyon shied away from them at first, but then they began hugging their loved ones with tears of joy in their eyes. We couldn't stop crying either. Jesus had healed all of them and we had seen every minute of it!

As Jesus walked by, the crowd made a path for him and stared at him with awe. They had never seen anything like this in their lives! We were staring in awe too! None of us had any doubts about what we had seen. These were true miracles. Jesus had healed all of them from this terrible disease of leprosy! We kept going over and over it in our minds.

The crowds began traveling back to their villages with their healed family and friends. They were laughing, shouting, and praising God! I had never observed such completely pure happiness in my life! As we were watching the happy crowd walk away and I felt a tap on my shoulder. I looked around and saw one of Jesus' disciples smiling at me. He began speaking and of course I couldn't understand what he was saying. Dr. Jenkins listened to him for a moment and nodded his head smiling at the man. After the man left, I turned to Dr. Jenkins. "What was he saying?" I said. "That was Simon Peter". He saw us follow Jesus down the path into the canyon. He's curious about who we are and invited us to his home for supper tonight. He said that Jesus would be there along with James and John. I told him we would be delighted to come."

What an opportunity! We were going to have some quality time with Jesus and his three favorite disciples. We had a light lunch and found a shady place to rest. We cleaned up the best that we could and made our way to Simon Peter's home. Peter had told Dr.

Jenkins how to find it. We approached the home about an hour and a half before sunset. Peter met us at the door and welcomed us in. It was a very small, plain house similar to others in the area. Peter introduced us to James, John, and Jesus. He showed us to a very low table where we were to recline on our left side, as was the custom in the area.

In a few moments, three women whom I assumed were the wives of the disciples and a fourth woman came in bringing the food. The food was a type of fish chowder along with some bread for us to dip into the chowder. The women poured what we believed to be wine into our goblets, but we quickly learned that it was a non-alcoholic grape juice. Jesus gave thanks to God for the food and we began eating. All of us had hearty appetites and the food soon disappeared. The women then brought in some grapes for us to eat after our main meal and then they sat away from the men.

Dr. Jenkins leaned over to me and told me that the fourth woman was Mary Magdalene. All of us observed her closely for the evening because of recent publications saying that Mary Magdalene was more than a friend to Jesus. There was not the slightest evidence of impropriety. James began telling a story and everyone in the room started laughing. Dr. Jenkins told me that James was telling about Jesus walking on the water and Peter getting out of the boat to walk on water to Jesus. Peter took a few steps and realized that he really was walking on water and began to sink like a rock. Jesus had to go pull him up. Everybody in the room including Jesus was laughing until tears rolled down their cheeks. Peter was even laughing at himself.

Peter asked where we were from and Dr. Jenkins said that we were from a far off land. After about two hours of companionship, we left Peter's home. Dr. Jenkins thanked everyone profusely for having us for supper. He asked if we could follow them while we were visiting the area and Peter said the equivalent of "of course."

Chapter 11

We spent the next two and a half weeks following Jesus and his disciples. We had a chance to actually meet several of the other disciples and their families. Dr. Jenkins was becoming more familiar with their language and was able to talk with them in simple terms. Of course they couldn't figure out his accent. All of them thought that we were strangers from a foreign land, except for Jesus. He didn't say anything, but I began to develop a feeling that perhaps he knew who we really were and where we were from. During the brief two and a half weeks, we saw Jesus teach in the temple. We saw him interacting with the scribes and Pharisees and frequently putting them in their places. We heard him quoting scripture from the book of Isaiah from memory. He quoted many other scriptures from the early Old Testament. It was obvious that he knew them extremely well. I had begun to be able to understand some of what he was saying and hearing the words spoken by Jesus himself went to the depth of my heart. We saw him perform miracle after miracle.

Our planned three-week visit went by in a flash. It was time for us to leave the holy land, yet none of us were ready to go. We couldn't get enough of seeing Jesus, but if we waited any longer, we risked not being able to leave at all. Our time machines' sophisticated equipment had to be used within the time frame that had been programmed into our computers prior to our original departure. So, we arose early on our last morning and began our trek back to our time machine.

I was very worried about getting back. I hadn't told the others, but going back home was going to be much more difficult. We would not have the help of global positioning satellites like we had when we started our journey. The slightest error could leave us isolated in space and time with no chance of recovery.

We located our travel machine with no difficulty. It didn't appear to have been disturbed. We removed the camouflage and began storing everything away. We didn't want to leave the slightest scrap behind. We had left some food on our craft and we began eating our last meal in the first century. As the others began their duties, I sat in the pilot's seat and began going through my checklist. I turned on the master power switch and there was no response. The control panel was dead! Frantically, I began flipping switches to no avail. Nothing! Absolutely nothing! The batteries had run down for some reason. Then I saw it. A secondary power switch had been left open. Our batteries were drained. We were stuck in the past!

I quickly began to search for solutions. Nothing worked. I became more and more frantic. We had to leave within a few hours at the most to fit into our time window. I tried everything that I could think of and nothing seemed to work. All of us began trying to find a solution with no results. Finally I turned to the others and suggested that we pray. Three weeks ago, I would never have even considered this. All of us got down on our knees and began to pray for guidance. Almost immediately, the answer came to me. We had some backup batteries for our cameras. We also had some small solar panels. We could jerry-rig them so that we would have enough power to start our small auxiliary engine. This in turn would generate enough power to start our main engines.

We quickly set everything up and we prayed again for success. Everything worked! Soon our engines were running properly and we were going over our checklists making sure that we were not off by even a millisecond. With a reluctant farewell to the Holy Land, we took off to return to the 21st century.

Before we knew it, we were back in the 21st century flying over Antarctica back to our landing area in South America where we made an uneventful landing. We leaped out of our travel machine and began slapping one another on the back. We couldn't wait to review the videos and the still pictures and show them to the world. Now there would be no lingering doubts. Everyone would accept Jesus as his or her Savior and Lord. The world would be a different place. There would be peace and love everywhere!

Chapter 12

Our travel back to Rio and then home seemed to take forever, but we finally arrived back in the United States and went straight to our hotel, carrying all of the camera equipment with us. We were prepared to make backup copies of everything. Soon the whole world would know what we knew. As we unpacked our video cameras, I turned on the first one to play the pictures we had reviewed before we left the Holy Land. As I waited for the pictures to play, I saw writing on the screen instead of pictures. The writing appeared to be in a foreign language. I called Dr. Jenkins and the others to come take a look.

Dr. Jenkins studied the words on the screen for a few minutes.

The words were:

Λεγει αυτω ο Ιησους οτι εωρακας με θωμα πεπιστενκας μκαριοι οι μή ιδοντες και πιστενσατες

Dr. Jenkins studied the words and said, "This is in ancient Greek!" It says, "Then Jesus told him 'You believe because you have seen me, but blessed are those who have not seen me and believe anyway.'" Dr. Covington was excited. He said, "That's John 20:29! It's what Jesus told Thomas after showing him the nail scars in his hands and the scar on his side!"

We frantically went through our cameras. Every picture that we had taken was gone and replaced with John 20:29! We stood staring at one another. Our proof was gone! Our trip had been for naught!

But then we knelt down and began to pray, asking for God's guidance. As we prayed, we were filled with a deep inner peace and happiness. We realized that even with our solid proof, there would always be those who doubted. When it came right down to it, everything still depended on faith. I was the modern doubting Thomas. I was the one who had to see the nail-scarred hands and see his side. I was the one who could not accept Jesus as my Lord and Savior without concrete proof.

I was saved by an unshakeable faith in Jesus Christ after seeing him in person. How much better would it have been if I could have had this faith without demanding proof. Now I was looking at Jesus and saying, "My Lord and my God!" I had no other proof to show anyone other than my own personal salvation through Jesus Christ, but that had been more than enough for millions of people over the past 2000 years. I now realized that each person's individual acceptance of Jesus Christ as their Savior would continue to be enough if we would just continue to spread the word to the four corners of the earth.

I had spent millions of dollars and a lot of time and energy looking for a truth that was right in front of me all the while. I now realized that even if we had been successful in bringing back movies of our experiences, people would still not have believed. They would have labeled them as fakes. When it came right down to it, I realized that the truth was right there in our Bibles all the time. All we had to do was look, read, pray, and believe.

Epilogue

We spent several days together praying and talking about what we had seen and heard. Then we returned to our respective homes. Each of us has become an eloquent proclaimer of the gospel throughout the world. Our experience had given us a passion similar to that of the early disciples. My friends have been amazed at the seemingly overnight change in my life.

We have been reuniting every six months to share our experiences and we are constantly in touch with one another by phone and e-mail. Our lives have been totally changed by meeting Jesus in person. But, most of all, we have been able to lead others to His wonderful salvation, which is a gift just for the asking. I had spent millions of dollars and a lot of time and energy over a period of years looking for the truth, only to find that the truth had always been there in front of me. It was right there in our Bibles all the time. The Holy Bible that I had once scorned is now one of the most important things in my life. All we have to do is look, read, study, and pray! What a wonderful feeling to know the depth of God's love for each of us! The knowledge that God sent his Son into the world for our salvation is the greatest thing we will ever know. It surpasses everything else in our lives.

Printed in the United States
62777LVS00001B/253-999